Hodder Toddler

This book belongs to:

....

For Christopher Melling
Thanks Dad

JUST LIKE MY DAD
by David Melling
British Library Cataloguing in Publication Data
A catalogue record of this book is available from the British Library.

ISBN 0 340 85198 8 (PB)

First edition published 2002
10 9 8 7 6 5 4 3 2 1

Published by Hodder Children's Books
a division of Hodder Headline Limited
338 Euston Road London NW1 3BH

Printed in Hong Kong

Just Like My Dad

David Melling

Hodder
Children's
Books

A division of Hodder Headline Limited

This is my dad.

One day, I'll have sharp teeth...

...just like my dad.

And spiky hair...

...just like my dad.

I'll grow long nails and a swishy tail...

...just like my dad.

and lick my nose...

...just like my dad.

When I eat my tummy talks...

gurgle
gurgle

Burp!

...just like my dad's.

And when I lie around being lazy my mum says...

My dad says
I must not be
afraid of
anything...

big...

...or small.

Sometimes my dad can be a little cross...

...but I can make him laugh really loud.

When we play
hide-and-seek with my
friends my dad likes to
go first...

...but he's not very good!

Even so, all my friends say,
when they grow up they want to be...

...just like my dad.

Goodbye
Hodder Toddler